Let's Get Active!

Let's Play Tag

Sara Milner

illustrated by

Joel Gennari

PowerKiDS press

New York

Published in 2018 by The Rosen Publishing Group, Inc.
29 East 21st Street, New York, NY 10010

First Edition

Managing Editor: Nathalie Beullens-Maoui
Editor: Melissa Raé Shofner
Art Director: Michael Flynn
Book Design: Raúl Rodriguez
Illustrator: Joel Gennari

Cataloging-in-Publication Data

Names: Milner, Sara.
Title: Let's play tag / Sara Milner.
Description: New York : PowerKids Press, 2018. | Series: Let's get active! | Includes index.
Identifiers: ISBN 9781538327364 (pbk.) | ISBN 9781508163862 (library bound) | ISBN 9781538327678 (6 pack)
Subjects: LCSH: Tag games–Juvenile literature.
Classification: LCC GV1207.M53 2018 | DDC 796—dc23

Manufactured in the United States of America

CPSIA Compliance Information: Batch #BW18PK. For further information contact Rosen Publishing, New York, New York at 1-800-237-9932

Contents

My family is going to the city park. We're going to play all day!

There are lots of kids at the park.

I know some of them from school.

My brother wants to play with his soccer ball.

Everyone else wants to play tag.

"Not it!" we all shout.

Everyone starts to run.

My brother is "it."

He chases us around the trees.

Everyone runs very fast.

My brother can’t tag us.

Watch out! I run right into
Megan's elbow.

We're okay, though.

My brother runs over.

He taps me on the back. “Tag, you’re it!”

I run as fast as I can.

We play tag all day.

Playing tag is lots of fun!
But it sure does make you tired!

Words to Know

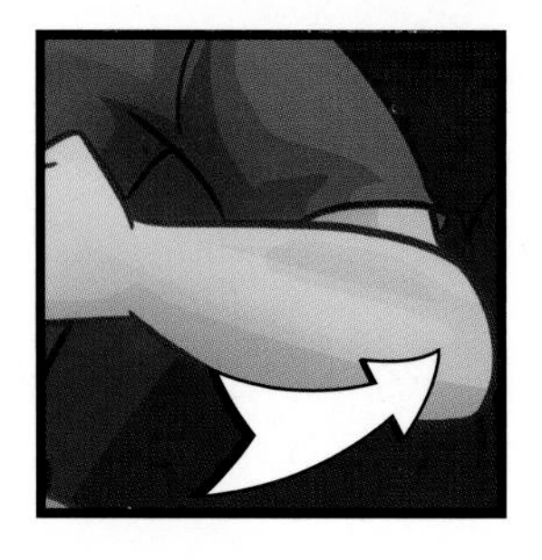

elbow

soccer ball

tree